LOVELAND PUBLIC LIBRARY

000557552

T3-AOR-211

1/20/16
$23.95

JN

Withdrawn

Major US Historical Wars

US-Led Wars
in Iraq
1991-Present

Jim Gallagher

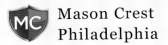

Mason Crest
Philadelphia

Mason Crest
450 Parkway Drive, Suite D
Broomall, PA 19008
www.masoncrest.com

© 2016 by Mason Crest, an imprint of National Highlights, Inc.

All rights reserved. No part of this publication may be reproduced or transmitted in any form or by any means, electronic or mechanical, including photocopying, recording, taping, or any information storage and retrieval system, without permission from the publisher.

Printed and bound in the United States of America.

CPSIA Compliance Information: Batch #MUW2015. For further information, contact Mason Crest at 1-866-MCP-Book.

3 5 7 9 8 6 4 2

Library of Congress Cataloging-in-Publication Data

ISBN: 978-1-4222-3358-0 (hc)
ISBN: 978-1-4222-8598-5 (ebook)

Major US Historical Wars series ISBN: 978-1-4222-3352-8

About the Author: Jim Gallagher is a freelance writer. He lives with his wife, LaNelle, and children Donald, Dillon, and Carin in Stockton, New Jersey.

Picture Credits: Central Intelligence Agency: 38 (left); OTTN Publishing: 9, 32 (left); used under license from Shutterstock, Inc.: 11, 20; Ken Tannenbaum / Shutterstock.com: 37; United Nations: 10, 31, 39, 41, 47; Thomas Hartwell/USAID: 50; U.S. Army photo: 51; U.S. Department of Defense: 1, 7, 24, 27, 28, 29, 30, 32 (right), 33, 35, 38 (right), 43, 45, 53 (bottom); U.S. Marine Corps photo: 48, 49; U.S. Navy photo: 13, 52, 53 (top); White House photo: 38 (center), 42.

Table of Contents

KEY ICONS TO LOOK FOR:

 Words to Understand: These words with their easy-to-understand definitions will increase the reader's understanding of the text, while building vocabulary skills.

 Sidebars: This boxed material within the main text allows readers to build knowledge, gain insights, explore possibilities, and broaden their perspectives by weaving together additional information to provide realistic and holistic perspectives.

 Research Projects: Readers are pointed toward areas of further inquiry connected to each chapter. Suggestions are provided for projects that encourage deeper research and analysis.

 Text-Dependent Questions: These questions send the reader back to the text for more careful attention to the evidence presented there.

 Series Glossary of Key Terms: This back-of-the book glossary contains terminology used throughout this series. Words found here increase the reader's ability to read and comprehend higher-level books and articles in this field.

Other Titles in This Series

Introduction

By Series Consultant Lt. Col. Jason R. Musteen

Lt. Col. Jason R. Musteen is a U.S. Army Cavalry officer and combat veteran who has held various command and staff jobs in Infantry and Cavalry units. He holds a PhD in Napoleonic History from Florida State University and currently serves as Chief of the Division of Military History at the U.S. Military Academy at West Point. He has appeared frequently on the History Channel.

Why should middle and high school students read about and study America wars? Does doing so promote militarism or instill misguided patriotism? The United States of America was born at war, and the nation has spent the majority of its existence at war. Our wars have demonstrated both the best and worst of who we are. They have freed millions from oppression and slavery, but they have also been a vehicle for fear, racism, and imperialism. Warfare has shaped the geography of our nation, informed our laws, and it even inspired our national anthem. It has united us and it has divided us.

Valley Forge, the USS *Constitution*, Gettysburg, Wounded Knee, Belleau Wood, Normandy, Midway, Inchon, the A Shau Valley, and Fallujah are all a part of who we are as a nation. Therefore, the study of America at war does not necessarily make students or educators militaristic; rather, it makes them thorough and responsible. To ignore warfare, which has been such a significant part of our history, would not only leave our education incomplete, it would also be negligent.

For those who wish to avoid warfare, or to at least limit its horrors, understanding conflict is a worthwhile, and even necessary, pursuit. The American author John Steinbeck once said, "all war is a symptom of man's failure as a thinking animal." If Steinbeck is right, then we must think. And we must think about war. We must study war with all its attendant horrors and miseries. We must study the heroes and the villains. We must study the root causes of our wars, how we chose to fight them, and what has been achieved or lost through them. The study of America at war is an essential component of being an educated American.

Still, there is something compelling in our military history that makes the study not only necessary, but enjoyable, as well. The desperation that drove Washington's soldiers across the Delaware River at the end of 1776 intensifies an exciting story of American success against all odds. The sailors and Marines who planted the American flag on the rocky peak of Mount Suribachi on Iwo Jima still speak to us of courage and sacrifice. The commitment that led American airmen to the relief of West Berlin in the Cold War inspires us to the service of others. The stories of these men and women are exciting, and they matter. We should study them. Moreover, for all the suffering it brings, war has at times served noble purposes for the United States. Americans can find common pride in the chronicle of the Continental Army's few victories and many defeats in the struggle for independence. We can accept that despite inflicting deep national wounds and lingering division, our Civil War yielded admirable results in the abolition of slavery and eventual national unity. We can celebrate American resolve and character as the nation rallied behind a common cause to free the world from tyranny in World War II. We can do all that without necessarily promoting war.

In this series of books, Mason Crest Publishers offers students a foundation for the study of American wars. Building on the expertise of a team of accomplished authors, the series explores the causes, conduct, and consequences of America's wars. It also presents educators with the means to take their students to a deeper understanding of the material through additional research and project ideas. I commend it to all students and to those who educate them to become responsible, informed Americans.

Loveland Public Library
Loveland, CO

Chapter 1

The Annexation of Kuwait

Early on the morning of August 2, 1990, a series of explosions rocked Kuwait City, the capital and largest city of the small kingdom of Kuwait. Military jets from the air force of Kuwait's larger neighbor, Iraq, dropped bombs and fired machine guns into government buildings and other strategic targets. Awakened by the violence, leaders of the small Persian Gulf emirate tried to find out what was happening. They soon received a chilling report: hundreds of Iraqi tanks and more than 100,000 well-trained soldiers had crossed the border and were moving toward the capital.

These members of Kuwait's military were unable to prevent the much larger Iraqi Army from overrunning the small emirate in July 1990.

There was no way Kuwait, a tiny desert kingdom of fewer than 2 million people, could repel an invasion by Iraq's military. Iraq had a population of more than 30 million in 1990, and possessed the largest army in the Middle East. Iraq's army had superior weapons and training, and many Iraqi soldiers were experienced combat veterans. Kuwait's small, lightly armed security force resisted just long enough to allow the country's ruler, Emir Jaber al-Ahmad al-Sabah, and most of his family to escape to Saudi Arabia. The fighting ended after just a few hours, with Iraq's dictator, Saddam Hussein, in control of Kuwait.

Kuwait was a valuable prize. Beneath the small country's desert sands lie enormous deposits of oil—according to some experts, more than 10 percent of the world's total. Oil is an important resource that is used to operate factories and produce electricity. Cars, trucks, airplanes, and ships all run on fuel processed from oil.

Iraq already possessed a large supply of its own oil, so the day's fighting gave Saddam Hussein control over approximately one-fifth of the world's oil supply. This made Iraq a potential threat to the United States and other countries with modern economies that depend on oil. Saddam could threaten to shut off the flow of oil if other countries did not agree with his actions. This would raise the price of oil, which in industrialized nations could cause an economic *recession* in which factories close and people lose their jobs. Twice during the 1970s, high oil prices had contributed to recessions. It had taken years for the United States to recover from the hard times.

 ## WORDS TO UNDERSTAND IN THIS CHAPTER

annex—to incorporate territory into the area ruled by a country.

recession—a period in which a country's economy shrinks or grows smaller, rather than growing larger. Usually a recession lasts for a limited time; an extended recession is known as a depression.

resolution—a formal expression of a decision by the United Nations Security Council, considered binding under international law.

This map of Iraq shows the location of its major cities, as well as the country's borders with Kuwait, Saudi Arabia, Jordan, and Turkey—all of which were important allies of the United States in 1990.

World leaders immediately condemned the Iraqi invasion of Kuwait. On August 3, in a special meeting room inside the United Nations building in New York City, representatives of 15 nations held an emergency session. The representatives were members of the U.N. Security Council, a powerful branch of the organization charged with maintaining world peace and security. The Security Council's rulings, known as **resolu-**

The U.N. Security Council votes on a resolution condemning Iraq's invasion of Kuwait in the summer of 1990. The U.N. Security Council's responsibilities include peacekeeping operations, the establishment of international sanctions, and the authorization of military action through resolutions.

tions, are considered to have the force of international law behind them. The U.N. Security Council voted unanimously to approve U.N. Security Resolution 660, which called for the "immediate and unconditional" withdrawal of Iraq from Kuwait.

Powerful leaders like U.S. President George H.W. Bush and British Prime Minister Margaret Thatcher also spoke out against Iraq's aggressive invasion. The Soviet Union, which had been Iraq's main provider of military supplies, suspended deliveries of weapons and equipment. Even the leaders of some other Arab countries, like Saudi Arabia and Egypt, spoke out against Saddam Hussein's conquest.

Despite the international opposition, Saddam Hussein believed no one would dare try to force him from Kuwait. After all, both the United States and the Soviet Union—considered the world's "superpowers" at the time— had been badly burned by involvement in foreign wars against seemingly weaker foes. During the 1960s and 1970s, nearly 60,000 American soldiers had been killed during the Vietnam War, and U.S. society had been bitterly divided over the unpopular conflict. The Soviet Union had been involved in a similar quagmire in Afghanistan from 1979 to 1989. The occupation of Afghanistan had weakened the U.S.S.R. By the summer of 1990 the Soviet Union was in the midst of major changes in its government and society. Saddam reasoned that despite their threats, the Americans and Soviets were bluffing. And if the superpowers did not take action, no other country would challenge Iraq's claim to Kuwait.

As president of Iraq, Saddam Hussein started wars against Iran (1980) and Kuwait (1990). He also used his military to repress Iraq's civilian population, killing hundreds of thousands of people. His efforts to acquire nuclear, chemical, and biological weapons led to repeated condemnation by the United Nations.

Saddam felt that the situation favored Iraq in other ways. Some Arab countries did not initially condemn the invasion of Kuwait, and the Iraqi dictator believed this meant the Arabs supported his actions. Also, if a war did come it would be fought over desert terrain that Iraqi forces knew better than anyone. Harsh and unfamiliar terrain could be used to great advantage against invaders—a painful lesson the Americans and Soviets had learned in Vietnam and Afghanistan.

The Iraqi dictator therefore responded to demands that he withdraw by issuing threats of his own. He promised to turn Kuwait City into a "graveyard," if any country attempted to challenge Iraq's takeover. He moved his troops closer to the border with Saudi Arabia, where they began constructing strong defenses. And on August 6 he declared that Iraq had officially *annexed* Kuwait.

Saddam Hussein was taking a risk by defying the world. But if his assessment of the situation was accurate, and there was no military response, Iraq would become a major player on the world scene. Iraq's proven military might would make the country the dominant power in the Middle East, while its increased share of the world's oil would give Iraq greater leverage over the United States and other Western nations that depended on the resource for their economies to operate. He had made his move; now the West had to decide how it would proceed.

 ## TEXT-DEPENDENT QUESTIONS

1. On what day did Iraq invade Kuwait?
2. Why was Iraq's conquest a potential threat to the United States and other western countries?
3. Why did Saddam Hussein believe that the United States and Soviet Union would not want to become involved in a war over Kuwait?

 ## RESEARCH PROJECT

Divide your school class into six groups, with each representing one of the five permanent members of the United Nations Security Council in 1990 (the United States, Soviet Union, China, France, and Great Britain), and one group representing Iraq. Students must do some research about the country in order to properly represent its interests and understand its positions. At a meeting of the Security Council, elect one person to lead the discussion, which should be set in August 1990. Question the Iraqi representative about his government's purpose for the invasion of Kuwait, and work together to try to develop a solution that—in the opinion of your teacher—would resolve the conflict without fighting.

Chapter 2

A Long Road to Conflict in Iraq

For most of Iraq's existence as a nation, its leaders had believed that Kuwait should be part of Iraq. But in reality, the emirate of Kuwait predated the creation of Iraq. The tiny kingdom had been declared in 1756, while the country of Iraq was not created until 1919, at the peace conference in Paris that ended the First World War, and did not become independent until 1936.

Iraq is located in a region known as Mesopotamia, where some of the world's earliest civilizations flourished more than 6,500 years ago. Around 500 years

American warships escort Kuwaiti oil tankers through the Persian Gulf to protect them from attack by Iranian forces during the Iran-Iraq War. The war was waged from 1980 to 1988. It left Iraq deeply in debt, and dictator Saddam Hussein hoped to improve his country's fortunes by seizing Kuwait in 1990.

ago, the region came under the control of the Ottoman Empire, a major world power that existed from the 15th century until the early 20th century. At the empire's height, the Ottoman rulers, known as sultans, ruled territories in North Africa, Central Asia, the Middle East, and Eastern Europe. The sultans were Muslims, and so were most of the people they ruled. However, because the empire was so widespread, it contained people of many different races and cultures. To rule effectively, the sultans had to create a strong system of local governments.

After Mesopotamia became part of the Ottoman Empire during the 16th century, it was divided into three *vilayets*, or provinces. The mountainous territory in the north was ruled from the city of Mosul. A central province was ruled from Baghdad. The southern province was ruled from the city of Basra. The sultans appointed *pashas*, or governors, to rule over

 # WORDS TO UNDERSTAND IN THIS CHAPTER

autonomous—politically independent and self-governing.

creditor—a country or person owed money by another.

economic sanctions—restrictions imposed to punish a country by preventing it from purchasing (or selling) goods and services.

glut—a larger supply of something than is needed.

mandate—the authority, granted by the League of Nations to an established power like Great Britain or France, to administer a less developed territory. Under the mandate system, the more established countries were expected to help the new nations develop good governments and the social institutions required for stability and independence.

nationalism—the desire by a people who share a language and culture to gain a politically independent state of their own.

protectorate—a country that is defended and controlled by a more powerful state.

stalemate—a situation in which neither of two opposing sides can win.

weapons of mass destruction (WMD)—weapons, such as biological or chemical agents or nuclear warheads, that are capable of killing large numbers of people.

the Mesopotamian *vilayets* and sent their troops to maintain control in the provinces.

The Ottoman Empire also claimed the Arabian Peninsula to the south and east. However, much of this territory was uninhabited desert, and there was no reason to appoint a governor or station troops there.

Around the year 1744, an Arab tribe known as the Bani Utub moved to an area of the Persian Gulf coast to the south of Basra. They established a small settlement at a sheltered harbor, which would one day become known as Kuwait City. In 1756, Sabah bin Jabir bin Adhabi became emir, or ruler, of this settlement, which became known as Kuwait. His descendants, the al-Sabah family, continue to rule the emirate today.

The Ottoman sultans considered Kuwait unimportant, so they allowed the al-Sabah family to rule the community in their name. The emir of Kuwait was expected to collect taxes for the Ottoman Empire and acknowledge the sultan's authority. Otherwise, the emirs maintained their *autonomy*.

Seeking Independence

During the 19th century, a movement called *nationalism* developed as groups of people who shared history, culture, and language began to contemplate breaking away from large empires. These national groups wanted to create countries of their own. However, imperial powers like the Ottomans, British, Russians, and French wanted to keep their vast empires intact. They arrested nationalist leaders and tried to stop their ideas from spreading.

One large national group within the Ottoman Empire was the Arabs, who lived in Mesopotamia and throughout the Arabian Peninsula. During the late 19th century, some Arab leaders began agitating for greater freedom. They wanted to create an independent Arab state that would stretch across the Middle East. The Ottoman sultans responded by repressing their Arab subjects.

When the Ottoman sultan started planning to build a railroad connecting Baghdad to Kuwait City, the al-Sabah emirs became concerned. They feared the railroad would permanently tie Kuwait to the Ottoman Empire. To maintain their freedom, they sought foreign help. They found an ally in Great Britain, which at the time was the world's most powerful country.

Britain's prosperity was due to its network of overseas colonies. The most important was British India, known as the "jewel of the empire." To maintain its empire, Britain needed to protect its ships as they traveled to and from the colonies. Britain was interested in the Persian Gulf because it was close to India. The British had friendly relations with Persia, on the other side of the Gulf, and had made treaties with several small Arab kingdoms in the southeastern Arabian Peninsula. British warships could stop for supplies at ports in these countries while patrolling the Indian Ocean and Red Sea. British leaders considered both Germany and the Ottoman Empire rivals for power. They believed the proposed German-Ottoman railroad to the Persian Gulf might one day enable Britain's enemies to threaten the sea route to India.

In 1899 Britain promised to ensure Kuwait's independence from the Ottoman Empire. In return, Kuwait's Emir Mubarak al-Sabah al-Sabah permitted the British to build a naval base in Kuwait. Although the Ottoman Empire never gave up its claim to Kuwait, it was unable to assert that claim while British warships patrolled the Gulf.

An Important Discovery

The Middle East became even more important to Britain after 1908, when vast quantities of oil were discovered in Persia. Oil could be used to operate modern factories and power the engines of trains, ships, automobiles, and airplanes. For Britain, the most important reason to be involved in the Persian Gulf was that the oil was necessary to fuel its warships.

In 1913 the emir of Kuwait signed a secret deal in which he promised to give Britain exclusive rights to develop any oil fields discovered in the country. To make this arrangement legal, Kuwait's murky status needed to be clarified. During the summer of 1913 the British negotiated an agreement with Ottoman Sultan Mehmed VI called the Anglo-Ottoman Convention. In this treaty, the British acknowledged that Kuwait was an autonomous Ottoman territory. In exchange, the sultan agreed not to interfere in Kuwait's internal affairs. This would allow Kuwait's leaders to sell oil to whomever they wanted.

The Anglo-Ottoman Convention never went into effect, however.

Before the treaty could be ratified, World War I broke out in Europe in August 1914. The Ottoman Empire soon entered the fighting on the side of Germany and Austria-Hungary (these became known as the Central Powers). Facing them were the Allied Powers, led by Great Britain, France, and Russia. With the Turks and British on opposite sides, Britain formally declared Kuwait an independent **protectorate**. The British also invaded Mesopotamia to protect the vital Anglo-Persian oil pipeline. By the time the Ottoman Empire asked for peace in October 1918, Britain controlled all of Mesopotamia as well as other Ottoman territories in the Middle East.

 ## OIL AND THE BRITISH NAVY

Before 1910, most British warships—particularly large battleships—were powered by coal. As fuel, coal had several drawbacks. It was bulky, so it required a lot of time and manual labor to load onto ships. Coal also took up a lot of valuable space within the ship itself. When engines that ran on diesel oil were developed, naval experts found they had many advantages. Oil could easily be pumped on board, reducing the amount of time and manpower needed to refuel. It could be stored anywhere within the hull and pumped to the engine, which led to improvements in ship designs. It also burned more efficiently than coal, so oil-fueled ships could travel farther and faster than coal-fueled vessels. In a time of war, these advantages would give oil-fueled ships a strategic edge.

The British Empire's prosperity depended on a strong navy that could protect shipping lanes and maintain the worldwide colonial empire. British leaders were interested in any new technology that would give their warships an advantage over their enemies. However, although the British Isles contained many coal mines, they had no oil fields. If the British navy committed to oil-fueled ships, it would need to find a supply of foreign oil that could easily be protected. Otherwise, if an enemy blocked Britain's access to oil the navy—and therefore the empire—would be helpless.

Despite this potential problem, in 1912 the British Navy decided to convert to oil-powered warships. Britain agreed to buy Persian oil, and began exploring Mesopotamia and Kuwait for other sources. Thus, oil provided a major reason for Great Britain to become involved in the politics of the Arab kingdoms in the Persian Gulf.

The Creation of Iraq

At the end of the war, the victorious Allies broke up the Ottoman Empire. During the war some Arabs had fought for the Allies, hoping they would be rewarded with the independent Arab state they had hoped for. Instead, the British and French divided Arab lands into small countries. One of these was Iraq, which was created from the Ottoman provinces of Mosul, Baghdad, and Basra. The Allied leaders claimed that Iraq and other new countries needed time to establish good governments and social institutions before they could become truly independent. They turned the problem over to the League of Nations, an organization created after the war to prevent future conflicts by enabling countries to settle disputes through negotiation and diplomacy. The League of Nations created a *mandate* system in which the new countries were placed under the control of a major power like Britain or France. Because of Iraq's strategic location and potential oil reserves, Britain asked for—and received—the mandate to rule Iraq.

Most Iraqis did not want to be ruled by Britain, or any other country for that matter. Iraqis also resented the borders imposed on them by the League of Nations. The border cut them off from Kuwait, which they argued should be part of their country, and limited Iraq's access to the Persian Gulf.

These problems were complicated by a history of hostility between the different ethnic groups in Iraq. Most of the people were Arabs, but in the north lived a group known as the Kurds. The Kurds' language and culture was different from the Arabs, and at the end of the war they had asked for their own country. When their request was refused by the League of Nations, some Kurds prepared to fight both the British and the Arabs for their independence.

Religion was also an issue. Most Iraqis are Muslims, but there are two major branches of this religion, Sunni Islam and Shia Islam. These two groups do not agree on how Islam should be practiced, and throughout history they have often fought bloody religious wars. Most Arabs in Mesopotamia followed Shia Islam, the main religion of Persia. However, the Ottoman sultans were Sunni Muslims, so during their rule Shiites were discriminated against and most government officials were Sunni Muslims. When the British set up Iraq's new government, the educated and experienced Sunni administrators were given a prominent role. This angered the Shiites.

Opposition to British rule, combined with ethnic and religious differences, caused revolts to erupt throughout Iraq in 1920. The British sent troops to put down the rebellion. However, occasional fighting occurred throughout the decade.

By the early 1930s, British leaders felt Iraq was ready for full independence. First, however, the League of Nations said that Iraq had to accept the border with Kuwait. In July 1932, Iraq's prime minister agreed to recognize the existing border, and the next month Iraq became independent. Despite the recognition, however, Iraqi leaders continued to covet the emirate. Iraq even threatened to annex Kuwait in 1961, although intervention by the British and the other Arab countries forced Iraq to back down from this threat.

In 1960, Iraq was a founding member of the Organization of Petroleum Exporting Countries (OPEC). A goal of OPEC was to control the international price of oil. To do this, each OPEC member agreed to a quota, or limit, on the amount of oil it would produce each year. In theory this would keep the supply of oil low, which would raise the price and ensure that OPEC members earned a significant profit.

Major Changes in the Middle East

The year 1979 was a momentous one in history. In the Middle East, two major government changes occurred. In Iraq, Saddam Hussein purged some of his political rivals from the Baath Party, which controlled the government. (The Arabic word *Baath* means "resurrection" or "renaissance," and the party was dedicated to promoting Arab nationalism and opposing the influence of Western countries in the Arab world.) Saddam had previously been a leading figure in the party; now he was the most powerful man in Iraq.

At around the same time, neighboring Iran was undergoing a violent change in government. The shah, or ruler, of Iran was unpopular during the 1970s, in part because his government used brutal tactics to maintain

Saddam Hussein viewed the Ayatollah Khomeini as a threat to his regime. After coming to power in 1979, Khomeini encouraged Shiites in other countries to rise up against their governments.

order. In late 1978, a Shiite Muslim leader named Ayatollah Ruhollah Khomeini inspired nationwide protests against the shah. In January 1979, the shah left the country, never to return. Khomeini and his supporters soon established a new government in Iran based on Islamic law.

Saddam Hussein saw the unrest in Iran as both a danger and an opportunity. Iraqis had always considered Iran a potential enemy. Iran was the largest country in the Persian Gulf region, with more than twice as many citizens as Iraq. Although Saddam Hussein and the leaders of the Baath Party were Sunni Muslims, a greater number of Iraqis followed the Shia branch of Islam. When Khomeini encouraged Shiites in other Gulf countries to rise up against their leaders, Saddam and the Baath Party felt threatened.

However, Khomeini had powerful enemies, including the United States, which had supported the shah's government in Iran. After radical Iranian students seized the U.S. embassy in Tehran and took its staff hostage, U.S. leaders imposed *economic sanctions* that were intended to isolate Iran and weaken Khomeini's regime. Saddam saw this as a chance for Iraq to replace Iran as the major regional power. In September 1980, Iraq's army invaded Iran.

Iraq's army was well trained and supplied with modern equipment—including some provided by the United States. It quickly captured 1,000 square miles of Iranian territory. However, the Iranian army regrouped and launched counteroffensives in 1981 and 1982 that recaptured most of the territory. By 1983, Iran and Iraq were at a *stalemate*. Iraq had better equipment, but Iran had more soldiers available. Neither country could win a decisive victory.

The Iran-Iraq War was one of the most brutal wars in modern history.

Both sides launched attacks against enemy civilians and against neutral ships in the Persian Gulf. Iraqi forces used deadly chemical weapons against Iranian soldiers. During the war, Saddam Hussein's military even used chemical weapons against his own citizens. Some Kurds had sided with the Iranians when they invaded northern Iraq, so when Iran was forced to withdraw, Saddam punished the rebellious Kurds. The most infamous gas attack occurred in March 1988, when more than 5,000 Kurdish civilians were killed in the village of Halabja. Dozens of other Kurdish villages in northern Iraq were also gassed or destroyed by the Iraqi military.

An Expensive War

Supplying an army during wartime is very expensive. Iraq spent $120 billion on the military between 1981 and 1985. At the same time, Iraq's oil revenues plunged from more than $26 billion a year in 1980 to less than $9 billion by 1982. To continue its war with Iran, Iraq borrowed billions of dollars from Kuwait, Saudi Arabia, and other Arab countries. The United States also loaned money to Iraq.

The Iran-Iraq War ended in August 1988, when the United Nations stepped in and negotiated a cease-fire. More than 600,000 Iranians and 375,000 Iraqis had been killed during the eight-year war, and over a million people had become refugees.

Iraq was in a desperate financial position when the war ended. It owed $77 billion to other countries, and it needed another $230 billion to rebuild its devastated cities and factories. But Iraq did not have enough money to rebuild and repay its debts. Most of the government's money went toward the military. Iraq could have saved billions for reconstruction by reducing the size of the army. However, Saddam was afraid to do this. Jobs were scarce, and unhappy, out-of-work soldiers might try to overthrow his government.

One way Iraq could raise more money would be to sell more oil. But during the 1980s new sources of oil had been found, and by 1988 there was an oil *glut*. Kuwait and the United Arab Emirates (UAE) made this problem worse by pumping more than their OPEC quotas. Because more oil was available than was needed, the price of oil had fallen sharply, from about $35 a barrel in 1982 to $15 a barrel in 1988. Iraq's oil minister estimated that the drop in price cost his country about $20 billion in revenue each year.

At an OPEC meeting in December 1988, Iraq asked for a higher quota so it could sell more oil. It also insisted that other OPEC members stop producing more than their own quotas, so the international price of oil would rise to a higher level. OPEC did agree to increase Iraq's quota slightly, but not as much as Saddam wanted. Meanwhile, Kuwait and the UAE continued to exceed their production quotas.

Iraq also sought relief from its crushing financial obligations. In February 1990, at a meeting of Arab leaders in Jordan, Saddam asked Iraq's **creditors** to forgive his country's debts. Iraq had prevented Iran's Shiite Islamic Revolution from spreading to Arab countries where Sunni Muslims held power, Saddam claimed, and the leaders of those countries could show their gratitude by writing off Iraq's debt. Despite this argument, Iraq's creditors still demanded their money.

Growing International Concerns

Meanwhile, the rest of the world was beginning to take a hard look at Iraq. In the United States, Saddam Hussein was criticized for his repression of the Kurds and his harsh treatment of political dissidents. He was condemned for using chemical weapons during the Iran-Iraq War. Experts worried that the dictator was developing other **weapons of mass destruction** as well.

It was common knowledge that Iraq wanted nuclear weapons. In 1981, Israeli warplanes had destroyed Iraq's Osirak nuclear reactor just before it was ready to start operating. The reactor would have been able to produce fuel for a nuclear bomb. During March 1990, British customs agents arrested five men who were trying to smuggle electrical switches to Iraq. The switches could be used to trigger a nuclear weapon. In April 1990, the British seized another illicit weapon-related shipment to Iraq. These incidents increased concerns about Iraq's WMD programs.

As international pressure mounted, Saddam became defiant. In April 1990, he declared that if Israel attacked Iraq again, he would launch chemical warheads against it. He also condemned Israel for its occupation of the West Bank and Gaza territories, which it had captured in a June 1967 war. Saddam also had harsh words for Israel's closest ally, the United States. He denounced "American imperialism," claiming that the United States wanted to dominate the Arabs because of their oil. Many Arabs considered the dictator a hero for standing up to the United States and Israel.

In May 1990, the Arab Leaque held a special meeting in Baghdad. The purpose of the meeting was to unite the Arab countries in condemning Israel. But during the conference, Saddam showed that he was also angry at the leaders of Gulf Arab states. He complained that the wealthy Arab states had refused to write off Iraq's debts, and he threatened military action against any OPEC country that continued to exceed its production quota.

Saddam repeated this threat privately at a July 16 OPEC meeting. He also claimed that during the Iran-Iraq War, Kuwait had stolen oil from Iraq's side of the Rumaila oil field, located on the border between the two countries.

On July 17, 1990, in a nationally televised speech, Saddam complained that Kuwait and the UAE had "stabbed Iraq in the back with a poisoned dagger." He said, "Instead of rewarding Iraq, which sacrificed the blossoms of its youth in the war to protect their houses of wealth, they are severely harming it." Saddam accused his neighbors of conspiring with the United States and Israel against Iraq, and he threatened military action. The next day, 30,000 Iraqi soldiers moved to the border with Kuwait.

Kuwait's ruler, Emir Jaber al-Ahmad al-Sabah, quickly asked other countries to help resolve the crisis. Egyptian president Hosni Mubarak offered to mediate the dispute. Mubarak met with Saddam Hussein on July 25, and the dictator promised that he would not attack unless the two sides were unable to resolve the crisis peacefully. The Egyptians arranged a peace conference in Saudi Arabia.

That same day, Saddam met with April Glaspie, the U.S. ambassador to Iraq. Saddam angrily presented Iraq's complaints against both Kuwait and the United States. Glaspie tried to calm him down, saying that the United States wanted a better relationship with Iraq. The ambassador was happy to learn about the proposed Egyptian peace conference. Shortly after the meeting, she told President George H. W. Bush that war could be avoided. However, Saddam may have misinterpreted some of Glaspie's comments as a sign that the United States would not intervene if Iraq attacked Kuwait.

On July 31 and August 1, emissaries from Iraq and Kuwait held talks in Saudi Arabia. However, even though Kuwait promised to stop overproducing oil and to forgive Iraq's war debts, the talks collapsed. At 2 A.M. on August 2, Iraq's army swept into Kuwait. Kuwait's small military was unable to stop the invasion. The emir and his family fled, and within a few hours Saddam Hussein controlled the country.

 ## TEXT-DEPENDENT QUESTIONS

1. When did Saddam Hussein become president of Iraq?
2. How many people were killed during the Iran-Iraq War?
3. What events during the spring of 1990 raised international concerns about Iraq's programs to develop weapons of mass destruction?

 ## RESEARCH PROJECT

Chemical weapons use toxic chemicals to incapacitate, harm, or kill others. They can be dispersed in gas, liquid, or solid forms. Due to their nature, chemical weapons often affect people other than their intended targets, and are considered weapons of mass destruction. They have been banned by many international treaties, most recently the 1993 Chemical Weapons Convention. Using the Internet or your school library, do some research on the two main types of chemical weapons (nerve agents and vesicant agents). What are the effects of each of these types of weapons? How large of an area or population can they affect? Write a two-page report, and include details about notable uses of these weapons in Iraq or elsewhere.

Chapter 3

The 1991 Gulf War and its Aftermath

The rest of the world reacted quickly to Iraq's invasion of Kuwait. Within a few hours, the United Nations Security Council had passed Resolution 660, which condemned the invasion and demanded the immediate withdrawal of all Iraqi forces from Kuwait. On August 6, the Security Council set up an economic *boycott* against Iraq (Resolution 661), and on August 9, it declared that any attempt by Iraq to annex Kuwait had "no legal validity, and would be considered null and void" under international law (Resolution 662).

George Bush, who was on vacation in Maine, publicly condemned the attack

An M-1A1 Abrams main battle tank lays a smoke screen while advancing during Operation Desert Storm, the military operation to drive Iraq out of Kuwait.

on August 2. "We call for the immediate and unconditional withdrawal of all the Iraqi forces," Bush said. "There is no place for this sort of naked aggression in today's world." The president halted American trade with Iraq, and ordered seven U.S. warships to be deployed to the Persian Gulf. Over the next few days, Bush spoke with key allies, including British Prime Minister Margaret Thatcher, Egyptian President Hosni Mubarak, and Soviet Premier Mikhail Gorbachev. Gradually, they began to formulate a response to Saddam's actions.

Because of the U.S. dependence on oil from Saudi Arabia, Bush felt it was necessary to defend the kingdom. His Secretary of Defense, Richard "Dick" Cheney, and top military advisor, Colin Powell, were sent to Saudi Arabia. They warned King Fahd and other Saudi leaders that an Iraqi attack might be imminent. Initially the Saudis did not want to allow foreign soldiers into their country. However, by August 7 they had agreed, and the first American soldiers were sent to Saudi Arabia. Operation Desert Shield, as the deployment became known, concentrated on fortifying defensive positions near the borders between Saudia Arabia and Iraq.

Experts agree that Saddam Hussein was surprised at the world's response. He did not believe anyone would challenge his conquest of Kuwait. On August 12, he declared that he would withdraw from Kuwait if Israel pulled out of the West Bank, Gaza Strip, and southern Lebanon. Saddam's proposal was *propaganda* that appealed to some people in the Arab world—particularly Palestinians in Israel, Jordan, Lebanon,

 # WORDS TO UNDERSTAND IN THIS CHAPTER

boycott—to prohibit business or social relations with a country as punishment for its policies or actions.

coalition—a temporary union between multiple countries to achieve a common goal.

propaganda—information, generally of a biased or misleading nature, that is used to further a particular political cause or point of view.

renounce—to formally declare abandonment of a claim, right, or possession.

These U.S. Marines were among the first troops sent to the Middle East, just days after the invasion of Kuwait. Their mission was to deter Saddam Hussein from attacking Saudi Arabia, a critical U.S. ally.

Syria, and other countries. However, the United States and its allies refused to negotiate with Saddam, insisting that Iraq withdraw immediately. As a result, on August 28 Saddam declared that Kuwait was officially the 19th province of Iraq, and renamed Kuwait City "Qadima."

On October 29, the U.N. Security Council passed Resolution 674. This said that if Iraq continued to ignore its demands to leave Kuwait, the U.N. would take further measures—including the possible use of military force—to remove the Iraqi army. The resolution also called for Iraq to pay a fine for the damages it had caused.

During this time, Bush negotiated with other world leaders to build a *coalition* of allies. Eventually, 34 nations joined the coalition, providing soldiers or financial support to the effort. The United States would provide the largest military force—by mid-November, 450,000 U.S. soldiers were stationed in the Persian Gulf. Saddam reacted by sending another 400,000 soldiers to Kuwait.

As the forces on both sides increased, war seemed increasingly likely. On November 29, the U.N. Security Council passed Resolution 678. The resolution established a deadline of January 15, 1991, for Iraq to withdraw from Kuwait. If Saddam refused, the United States and its allies were authorized to use military force to free Kuwait.

The deadline passed with Iraqi forces still occupying the country. At 3 A.M. on January 17, coalition air forces attacked Baghdad. The 1991 Gulf War had begun. Over the next five weeks, coalition airstrikes destroyed strategic targets in Iraq and Kuwait, including government buildings, electrical plants, radar stations, and Scud missile launchers.

With Saddam's defenses weakened, a ground assault began on February 24. U.S., British, and French tank divisions penetrated deep into Iraq, while U.S. Marines and a force made up of Egyptians, Syrians, and soldiers from other Arab countries pushed into Kuwait. The coalition forces routed the overmatched Iraqi army. As the Iraqis retreated from Kuwait, they left a trail of dead soldiers and burning vehicles on the main highway. Television stations broadcast pictures of the carnage along the

Iraqi soldiers surrender to the 1st U.S. Marine Division on February 26, the third day of the ground offensive phase of Operation Desert Storm.

These Iraqi military vehicles were destroyed by coalition aircraft while Iraq's army was retreating from Kuwait.

infamous "Highway of Death." By February 27, the U.N. coalition had achieved its objective—forcing the Iraqi army from Kuwait.

Some people wanted the coalition to continue on to Baghdad and over-throw Saddam Hussein. However, the United Nations had only author-ized the coalition to free Kuwait. Also, Arab members of the coalition, such as Saudi Arabia and Egypt, opposed a full-scale invasion of Iraq. Thus, the decision was made to halt the attack. On February 28, about 100 hours after the ground war began, President Bush declared a cease-fire. But he encouraged Iraqi citizens to rise up and overthrow their oppressive dictator.

On March 2, the Security Council set the conditions for peace. Under U.N. Security Council Resolution 686, Iraq had to **renounce** its claim to Kuwait, return all Kuwaiti property seized during the occupation, account for Kuwaiti prisoners, provide information about the location of mines and other weapons in Kuwait, and accept financial responsibility for the damage caused by the invasion. Resolution 687 established the border

General Norman Schwarzkopf planned the highly successful Desert Storm offensive that liberated Kuwait.

between Iraq and Kuwait and set up a demilitarized buffer zone between the two countries. Most importantly, this resolution ordered Iraq to terminate its chemical, biological, and nuclear weapons programs.

On March 3, in a meeting at Safwan, Iraq, Saddam Hussein agreed to abide by the U.N. resolutions. In return, the coalition did not impose strict terms on the defeated nation. The core of Iraq's army was not disbanded, and kept its helicopters and other weapons.

This would prove to be a costly mistake. Responding to U.S. encouragement, the Shiites in southern Iraq rebelled against the government in March of 1991. But because Saddam still had control of his army, he was able to use it to brutally suppress the Shiite rebels. The army then moved north to put down a revolt among Iraq's Kurds in April, forcing hundreds of thousands of Kurds to flee their homes. Both Shiites and Kurds felt betrayed by the United States, which had done nothing to support their uprisings.

The United Nations moved belatedly to condemn Saddam's attacks on his own people. U.N. Security Resolution 688 condemned Iraq's repression of its civilian population. On April 7, to protect the Kurds, coalition aircraft began patrolling a "no-fly zone" over northern Iraq. A second no-fly zone was established over southern Iraq in August 1992. The no-fly zones helped reduce attacks by Saddam's forces in the Kurdish and Shiite regions.

The Search for Weapons

A special commission, called UNSCOM, was formed to make sure Iraq complied with the United Nations order to destroy its weapons of mass destruction. The process of disarmament was supposed to be completed in 105 days. However, Iraqis tried to hamper UNSCOM efforts to find and destroy the prohibited weapons. In one incident during June 1991, Iraqi soldiers fired at UNSCOM inspectors when they tried to stop a convoy of Iraqi trucks. (The trucks had been carrying equipment related to Iraq's nuclear weapons program, which was later seized and destroyed.) In another incident, when UNSCOM inspectors discovered a cache of important documents relating to Iraq's nuclear program, Iraqi officials tried to confiscate the documents. Iraqi leaders also told UNSCOM that the country did not have a biological weapons program. Later, after UNSCOM found evidence of the program, the Iraqis changed their story, claiming the biological weapons had been intended for "defensive military purposes."

Over the next several years, Iraq's attempts to obstruct UNSCOM led to additional U.N. resolutions condemning the country. The United Nations also tried to pressure Iraq to comply with its resolutions by maintaining the economic sanctions which had been imposed immediately after the invasion of Kuwait. However, the effect of the sanctions was to make it harder for ordinary Iraqis to get food and medicine.

A U.N. team was assigned to find Iraq's chemical, biological, and nuclear weapons, and dispose of warheads such as the ones pictured here in the summer of 1991. However, Iraqi authorities refused to cooperate with the inspectors and tried to hide elements of their WMD programs.

(Top) U.S. Air Force F-15 Eagles fly a routine patrol mission over Southern Iraq as part of Operation Southern Watch, which protected Shiite areas in southern Iraq from 1997 to 2003. Another mission, Operation Northern Watch, prevented Saddam from attacking the Kurdish communities in northern Iraq during the same period.

Despite the lack of cooperation, between 1992 and 1997 UNSCOM inspectors shut down Iraq's nuclear program and destroyed much of its chemical and biological arsenal. But although inspectors estimated they had found 90 percent of Iraq's WMD, they believed some weapons might be hidden in areas they had not been permitted to search. They wanted to search Saddam's royal palace complexes, which included thousands of buildings.

Iraq refused to allow UNSCOM to inspect Saddam's palaces. In October 1997, the Iraqi government accused an American member of the UNSCOM team, Scott Ritter, of being a spy for the United States and Israel. They forced the American inspectors to leave Iraq.

The crisis over weapons inspections in Iraq continued into 1998. At a speech at the Pentagon, U.S. President Bill Clinton said, "It is obvious that there is an attempt here ... to protect whatever remains of [Iraq's] capacity to produce weapons of mass destruction, the missiles to deliver them, and the feedstocks necessary to produce them. The UNSCOM inspectors believe that Iraq still has stockpiles of chemical and biological munitions, a small force of Scud-type missiles, and the capacity to restart quickly its production program and build many, many more weapons." In October, Clinton signed the Iraqi Liberation Act. This legislation made removing Saddam Hussein and establishing a democratic government in Iraq part of U.S. foreign policy. However, although the U.S. promised $97 million to Iraqi groups opposed to Saddam, the legislation did not permit the U.S. military to overthrow the regime. After passage of this act, Saddam refused to cooperate with UNSCOM.

The United States and Great Britain threatened military action to force Iraq to comply with the United Nations. After discussion with U.N. Secretary-General Kofi Annan, Saddam agreed to let the inspections resume in November 1998. However, when UNSCOM chief Richard Butler reported that Iraqis were still interfering, the U.N. inspectors left Iraq in December.

On December 16, 1998, military forces from the United States and Great Britain launched Operation Desert Fox, a four-day bombing campaign against Iraq. U.S. President Bill Clinton explained that the purpose of the airstrikes was to "designed to degrade Saddam's capacity to devel-

Gen. Anthony C. Zinni, commander of U.S. military forces in the Persian Gulf region, discusses the result of Operation Desert Fox in a briefing at the Pentagon, December 21, 1998.

op and deliver weapons of mass destruction, and to degrade his ability to threaten his neighbors." Critics of Clinton's administration viewed the attack as a way to distract attention from the president's impending impeachment, which occurred December 19.

Operation Desert Fox was a military success—more than 75 sites in Iraq were destroyed. However, in the long term the airstrikes failed to change Iraq's stance toward the inspection program. When the bombing ended, Saddam Hussein refused to let the U.N. inspectors back into Iraq.

In addition, many nations were growing concerned about the effect sanctions were having on the people of Iraq. In 1999, three of the five permanent members of the U.N. Security Council—France, Russia, and China— called for disbanding UNSCOM and lifting the sanctions. By the end of the year a new monitoring organization, the U.N. Monitoring, Verification, and Inspection Commission (UNMOVIC) had replaced UNSCOM. However, the sanctions remained in place, and for the next four years Saddam Hussein refused to allow U.N. inspections.

 ## TEXT-DEPENDENT QUESTIONS

1. What was the purpose of U.N. Security Council Resolution 661, passed in August 1990?
2. The ground war phase of Operation Desert Storm began on February 24, 1991. How long did it last?
3. What was the purpose of Operation Desert Fox?

 ## RESEARCH PROJECT

Using the Internet or your school library, learn more about the world leaders who were involved in the decision to go to war against Iraq in 1991, such as George H.W. Bush, Margaret Thatcher, Mikhail Gorbachev, Hosni Mubarak, or King Fahd. Write a two-page report about this leader's political career and accomplishments. Share your report with the class.

Chapter 4

The 2003 Iraq War

O n January 20, 2001, George W. Bush became the nation's 43rd president. Bush was the oldest son of the president who had managed the 1991 Gulf War so successfully. The new president selected several of his father's former advisors for important positions in his government. Bush had chosen Dick Cheney to run with him as vice president, and after the election he appointed Colin Powell to serve as U.S. Secretary of State.

For the first nine months of his term, Bush maintained the existing U.S. policy toward Iraq. This "containment" policy involved patrolling the no-fly zones to

Secretary of Defense Donald Rumsfeld (left) meets with President George W. Bush and Vice President Dick Cheney to discuss the "war on terrorism." The American leaders soon determined that Iraq posed a potential danger to the United States that required the removal of Saddam Hussein from power.

keep Saddam from moving his army, and working through the United Nations to maintain sanctions until Iraq disarmed.

Things changed radically, however, on September 11, 2001, when Muslim terrorists hijacked airplanes and crashed them into the World Trade Center in New York City and the Pentagon near Washington, D.C. More than 3,000 Americans were killed in these terrorist attacks. In response, President Bush soon declared a "war on terrorism." He warned that the United States would not only destroy terrorist groups, it would also target any country that helped them.

Bush's first target was al-Qaeda, a shadowy organization which U.S. leaders believed had planned the September 11 attacks. A renegade Saudi millionaire named Osama bin Laden had created the group during the early 1990s. Bin Laden, a devout Muslim, had become angry at the West during the 1990–91 Gulf crisis. Mecca, the holiest shrine in Islam, is located in Saudi Arabia, and bin Laden was offended by the presence of U.S. troops near the sacred land. Soon, bin Laden and his followers were training terrorists and encouraging attacks against Western targets, hoping to drive American soldiers out of the Middle East.

In 1996, Bin Laden had established a base in Afghanistan, where al-Qaeda operated training camps with the protection and support of the government. After the September 11 attacks, the United States insisted that Afghanistan arrest and hand over the terrorist leader, but the Afghan government refused. In October 2001, the U.S. and its allies invaded Afghanistan. They soon overthrew the country's repressive government,

 WORDS TO UNDERSTAND IN THIS CHAPTER

preemptive war—a conflict that begins in order to defeat or prevent a perceived threat before it can materialize. Starting a war before an attack has occurred is not permitted under the United Nations charter, unless it is authorized by the U.N. Security Council beforehand.

proscribe—to make something illegal.

disrupted the al-Qaeda terrorist camps, and forced bin Laden into hiding.

Few people were surprised by this invasion, and most of the world sympathized with the United States. The General Assembly of the United Nations had officially condemned the terrorist attacks on September 12, while the Security Council reaffirmed two resolutions that had been pased before the attacks occurred Resolutions 1267 (October 1999) and 1333 (December 2000) demanded that Afghanistan turn over Osama bin Laden and shut down his terrorist camps. Great Britain, Australia, and other U.S. allies participated in the attack on Afghanistan, and dozens of other countries supported the "war on terrorism."

U.S. leaders used the September 11 terrorist attack on the World Trade Center and Pentagon to justify a new policy known as the Bush Doctrine: attacking potential threats before they could menace the United States.

Target: Iraq

But even before the fighting in Afghanistan was finished, U.S. leaders were developing plans to deal with other potentially dangerous nations. Soon, President Bush's advisors were divided into two camps. A few, like Colin Powell, believed the best way to contain potential threats was by working through the United Nations, using diplomacy and economic sanctions. Others proposed a radical new approach. Secretary of Defense Donald Rumsfeld and his top deputy, Paul Wolfowitz, advocated a new policy: the United States should strike at potential threats before it was attacked. This policy of ***preemptive war***, which Vice President Cheney also supported, seemed contrary to the U.N. charter, which forbade countries from attacking each other. However, Cheney, Rumsfeld, and

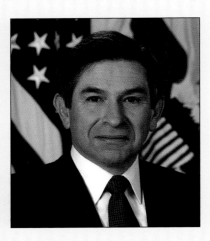

Three of George W. Bush's closest advisors pressed the president to invade Iraq. Both CIA Director George Tenet (left) and National Security Advisor Condoleezza Rice (center) told the president in 2002 that Iraq possessed weapons of mass destruction. Deputy Secretary of Defense Paul Wolfowitz (right) helped to develop the policy of preemptive war.

Wolfowitz argued that such a strike, done to prevent an impending attack, could be considered self-defense rather than an aggressive war.

Eventually, Bush embraced the concept of preemptive war, which became part of a new policy called the Bush Doctrine. Another element of the Bush Doctrine said that the United States would act to defend itself against potential threats, even if its allies or the international community did not support the use of force.

The Bush administration soon identified three countries as potential threats: Iran, North Korea, and Iraq. U.S. intelligence agents believed that all three countries were trying to develop nuclear weapons. All three had also assisted terrorists in the past, although none had been associated with al-Qaeda. In fact, although the first Gulf War had helped to inspire the creation of al-Qaeda, Osama bin Laden refused to have anything to do with Saddam Hussein. Bin Laden wanted to replace secular rulers in the Middle East with governments that interpreted and followed Islamic law. He considered Saddam an enemy of Islam, and encouraged Muslims to overthrow his regime.

Despite the lack of a connection between al-Qaeda and Iraq, Bush and his advisors argued that the logical next step in the "war on terrorism" was to remove Saddam Hussein from power. In 2002, the Department of

Defense began drawing up plans for an invasion of Iraq. The government also began a public-relations campaign to convince the world that an attack was justified. Administration officials said they had secret evidence proving the existence of Saddam Hussein's WMD programs. They discussed a potential scenario in which a terrorist smuggled an Iraq-built nuclear bomb or chemical weapon into a U.S. city. In September 2002, National Security Advisor Condoleezza Rice told CNN, "We don't want the smoking gun to be a mushroom cloud." In October, Congress passed a resolution giving President Bush authority to "defend the national security of the United States against the continuing threat posed by Iraq."

U.S. leaders also put pressure on the United Nations. They argued that the U.N. would become irrelevant if it did not force Saddam Hussein to comply with the 16 Security Council resolutions that had been passed since 1991. On September 12, 2002, President Bush presented the U.S. case against Iraq to the U.N. General Assembly. Bush claimed that Iraq had developed weapons of mass destruction, and pointed out that the U.N. Commission on Human Rights had accused the Baath regime of "extremely grave" violations in 2001. He also tried to link Saddam to international terrorism. "Iraq continues to shelter and support terrorist organizations," he said. "And al-Qaeda terrorists escaped from Afghanistan are known to be in Iraq." In his speech, Bush implied that the United States was prepared to attack Iraq to enforce past U.N. resolutions—even if the U.N. did not support such an attack.

Mohamed el-Baradei (left) and Hans Blix address the media at a press conference in November 2002, shortly after the U.N. Security Council voted to return the weapons inspection teams to Iraq.

Over the next eight weeks, the Security Council debated what to do about Iraq. In the meantime, Iraq responded by denying the charges that it was operating WMD programs or had sheltered al-Qaeda terrorists. In late September and early October, Iraqi leaders met in Vienna with Hans Blix, executive director of UNMOVIC, and Mohamed el-Baradei, director general of the International Atomic Energy Agency (IAEA). The Iraqis agreed to permit U.N. inspections to resume immediately.

On November 8, 2002, the U.N. Security Council approved Resolution 1441. The resolution declared that Iraq had not conformed to previous Security Council resolutions, and offered the country "a final opportunity to comply with its disarmament obligations." Iraq was given 30 days to present a complete report on its WMD programs. As had been agreed in Vienna, inspectors from UNMOVIC and the IAEA were to be given complete and immediate access to any site in Iraq they wished to inspect. The Security Council warned that any violation of these conditions would result in "serious consequences."

Inspections Resume

Ten days after the resolution was passed, UNMOVIC and IAEA teams resumed inspections in Iraq for the first time in four years. Iraq also filed a 12,000-page declaration of all its weapons programs just before the December deadline called for in Resolution 1441. However, many experts believed that the report had failed to fully account for Iraq's *proscribed* weapons programs. El-Baradei told the U.N. that Iraq's report "did not provide any new information relevant to certain questions that have been outstanding since 1998."

Over the next two months, the inspectors had made some disturbing discoveries. Inspectors found 11 artillery shells which had not been declared in the December report. The shells could be used to carry chemical agents, although they were empty. Iraqi leaders dismissed them as old weapons that had been accidentally overlooked. They released documents that had not been included in the December 7 report, indicating that many similar shells had already been destroyed. The inspectors, however, believed the warheads were new. In addition, the inspectors found thousands of hidden documents related to weapons programs, which should

U.S. Secretary of State Colin Powell speaks to the U.N. Security Council about evidence the United States had developed indicating that Iraq was continuing to produce weapons of mass destruction. Much of the information that Powell reported turned out to be inaccurate.

have been turned over to the U.N. Finally, a number of Iraqi scientists had refused to speak with inspectors. Although the Iraqi government insisted that it had ordered the scientists to cooperate, U.S. spies reported that the scientists had been warned they would be executed if they spoke with the inspectors. On January 27, 2003, Hans Blix told the Security Council, "Iraq appears not to have come to a genuine acceptance, not even today, of the disarmament which was demanded of it."

On February 5, 2003, Colin Powell spoke to the United Nations. He used U.S. intelligence reports—several of which later turned out to be wrong—in an effort to prove that Saddam Hussein was still trying to fool the U.N. inspectors. He said that war was justified because of Iraq's WMD program, along with Saddam's human rights abuses and support of terrorism. He argued that the U.N. should support a war against Iraq. "The issue before us is not how much time we are willing to give the inspectors to be frustrated by Iraqi obstruction," said Powell. "But how much longer are we willing to put up with Iraq's noncompliance before we, as a council, we, as the United Nations, say: 'Enough, enough.'"

The Security Council was not convinced. France, Russia, China, and other nations insisted that Resolution 1441 did not automatically authorize war. Despite this opposition, U.S. and British leaders began preparing for a military intervention in Iraq. They began to enlist other countries to join them in forcing Saddam Hussein from power. Spain, Japan, Australia, and South Korea offered support, as did dozens of smaller countries. Bush referred to these countries as the "coalition of the willing." However, some critics complained that the United States had essentially bribed these allies by offering financial incentives, trade agreements, or other valuable concessions in exchange for their support.

Most people outside of the United States—and many U.S. citizens as well—opposed war with Iraq. Protests and peace marches were held in New York, London, Paris, Tokyo, and other major cities. Crowds of angry Muslims burned American flags to protest U.S. policies in the Middle East. Critics of the Bush administration argued that Iraq was a diversion from the "war on terrorism." Many believed the United States simply wanted to seize control of the country's oil.

A Deadline for War

In February, the United States and Great Britain proposed a new resolution stating that Iraq had failed to meet its obligations under Resolution 1441. This would clear the way for war. France, Russia, China, Germany, and other countries opposed this new resolution. They wanted to let the U.N. inspectors continue their work. UNMOVIC and IAEA reports from February and early March had indicated that the inspectors were making progress, but that more time was needed. U.S. and British leaders believed Iraq had already been given enough time. Amid bitter disagreement, the draft resolution was withdrawn.

The United States and Britain claimed that because Iraq was a threat

Soon after the war began, President Bush addressed the nation from the White House. "At this hour, American and coalition forces are in the early stages of military operations to disarm Iraq, to free its people and to defend the world from grave danger," Bush said. "These are opening stages of what will be a broad and concerted campaign."

U.S. Marines captured enemy prisoners of war to a holding area in the desert of Iraq on March 21, 2003, during Operation Iraqi Freedom.

to their security, they did not need U.N. permission to remove Saddam. On March 17, 2003, Bush gave Saddam Hussein 48 hours to leave Iraq. When Saddam was still there on March 20, the coalition launched the Iraq War.

At about 5:30 a.m. on the morning of March 20—some 90 minutes after Bush's deadline had passed—a series of explosions rocked Baghdad. People in the city were awakened by the sound of air-raid sirens, as bombs and jet-propelled cruise missiles slammed into buildings. The Iraq War had begun.

Unlike the previous Gulf War, this time the coalition's war plans called for a ground invasion to begin at the same time as the aerial attacks. Over the next three weeks, U.S. tanks and infantry raced across the desert toward Baghdad, while British troops captured strategic cities and oil fields in southern Iraq. On April 9, U.S. troops entered Baghdad, forcing Saddam and his government to flee. Americans helped Iraqis pull down enormous statues of the dictator, to show that Saddam's power had ended.

The collapse of Saddam Hussein's government occurred so quickly that U.S. forces were not prepared to step in immediately and maintain order. People throughout Iraq celebrated the fall of the regime in early April, but these celebrations soon turned into rioting in Baghdad, Mosul, Basra, and other cities.

As Iraq's government collapsed, there was no longer an army or police force to preserve order in the cities. U.S. soldiers tried to protect electrical plants, water facilities, and oil pipelines, but there were not enough troops to prevent looting and violence. Priceless treasures were stolen from museums, and banks were robbed. Armed gangs roved city streets, making it unsafe for civilians to leave their homes. Soon, crowds began to gather to protest the U.S. occupation of Iraq. In many cases, Muslim religious leaders, both Sunni and Shiite, incited the protesters.

 ## TEXT-DEPENDENT QUESTIONS

1. What Middle Eastern country allowed Osama bin Laden to establish a base and operate al-Qaeda training camps from 1996 until 2001?
2. Which Deputy Secretary of Defense helped to develop the policy of preemptive war?
3. What are some of the reasons that U.S. Secretary of State believed the United Nations should support a war to remove Saddam Hussein from power?

 ## RESEARCH PROJECT

A number of George W. Bush's top advisors, including Dick Cheney, Colin Powell, and Paul Wolfowitz, had previously been involved in the 1991 Gulf War. Using the Internet or your school library, learn more about these advisors. Choose one, and write a two-page report about his role in the 1991 and 2003 conflicts. Share your report with the class.

Chapter 5

Fighting an Insurgency in Iraq

O n May 1, 2003, President George W. Bush declared the end of "major combat operations." However, this announcement, made on the deck of an American aircraft carrier in front of a large banner that read "mission accomplished," turned out to be premature.

Although many Iraqis were thankful to see Saddam gone, they resented the presence of coalition troops. Some Sunni Muslims began to wage an *insurgency* against the soldiers occupying the country. Resistance fighters launched

An American soldier mans an M-240 machine gun while patrolling the city of Fallujah, where a major battle was fought against Sunni insurgents during 2004.

surprise attacks against U.S. patrols. Homemade bombs were used to blow up security checkpoints, military convoys, and civilian targets. The Bush administration claimed that attacks were the work of a small number of Baath Party supporters or Saddam loyalists. However, when U.S. soldiers arrested suspected insurgents, more Iraqis became angry and joined the rebels. Reports that American soldiers had tortured and humiliated Iraqis detained at the Abu Ghraib prison in Baghdad also inflamed many Muslims.

The Sunni insurgents also targeted Iraqi Shiites. Shiites retaliated, carrying out murderous violence against their Sunni neighbors. Shiite militias also battled American soldiers. One of the largest of these was the Mahdi Army, led by a Shiite cleri named Moqtada al-Sadr. During April 2004, the Mahdi Army launched attacks on U.S. bases in a Shiite neighborhood in Baghdad, as well as in other Shiite strongholds such as Karbala, Kufa, Kut, and Najaf. Ultimately, the American and Iraqi government forces regained control of the territories, and Moqtada al-Sadr agreed to stop fighting the U.S. forces.

In addition to these problems, foreign fighters slipped into Iraq and carried out indiscriminate attacks against civilians. They hoped to foment a civil war and thereby make Iraq ungovernable. Some of these people were linked to the terrorist organization al-Qaeda, including Abu Musab al-Zarqawi. Zarqawi became the leader of a group that called itself al-Qaeda in Iraq, and he advocated for Sunnis to kill Shiites.

As the insurgency continued, the Coalition Provisional Authority

 WORDS TO UNDERSTAND IN THIS CHAPTER

insurgency—a rebellion or uprising against a government.

surge—a sudden, powerful movement. During the Iraq War, the term was used to refer to a large increase in the number of American troops serving in the country, in order to provide security in Baghdad, Anbar province, and other areas where rebel groups were fighting.

American L. Paul Bremer (left) served as administrator of the Coalition Provisional Authority (CPA), which was formed on April 21, 2003, to govern Iraq until a new national government could be formed. British diplomat Sir Jeremy Greenstock (right) worked closely with the CPA as the United Kingdom's Special Representative to Iraq. The Coalition Provisional Authority was dissolved on June 28, 2004, when an Iraqi interim government headed by prime minister Iyad Allawi was created.

(CPA)—the transitional government set up by the U.S. after the overthrow of Saddam Hussein—was blamed for many problems. Electrical power was spotty in many places, and people had to wait in long lines for food, clean water, gasoline, and other necessities. The CPA pointed to its accomplishments—rebuilding schools and hospitals; connecting water, power, and telephone lines; clearing harbors and canals; and other projects. However, the slow pace of reconstruction angered many Iraqis, leading to protests. In the United States, meanwhile, critics complained that the Bush administration had created a detailed plan to win the war, but it had not properly planned how to rebuild Iraq.

In the spring of 2004, an increasing number of insurgent attacks on Americans and Iraqis who supported the CAP led the American military to send U.S. Marines to the city of Fallujah. During the month of April, the Marines battled insurgents throughout the city. It was the largest battle in Iraq since Bush had declared the end of the war a year earlier. Insurgents also launched attacks in Ramadi, the capital of Al Anbar province, hoping to divert American soldiers away from Fallujah. The fighting finally ended

U.S. Marines fire at enemy targets in Fallujah during Operation Al Fajr in November 2004.

in early May, when the Marines turned control of Fallujah over to an Iraqi police force.

The battles in Fallujah and Ramadi marked a major change in Americans' perception of the war. Until Fallujah, the U.S. government had claimed that the insurgency would die out as Saddam's few supporters acknowledged that he was never going to return as Iraq's leader. The brutal house-to-house fighting in Fallujah and the attacks in Ramadi revealed that there were more insurgents in Iraq than anyone had previously realized, and that they were very determined in their opposition to the U.S. occupation of Iraq.

Unfortunately, the Iraqi force tasked with maintaining peace in Fallujah soon broke apart, and many of its weapons fell into the hands of insurgent groups. This required the Marines and U.S. Army to return to Fallujah in November 2004, where they fought the largest battle of the entire Iraq War. The insurgents, as well as terrorists from other countries who had come to fight the Americans, hid booby traps and bombs throughout the city. They established defensive positions and towers where snipers could fire on American troops. More than 13,000 American, British, and Iraqi troops were sent to Fallujah, and it took nearly two months of heavy fighting in the streets of the city before the insurgents were defeated.

WMD Discoveries and a War Crimes Trial

As soon as Baghdad was captured in April 2003, inspectors began looking for Iraq's weapons of mass destruction. The Iraq Survey Group (ISG),

A precision air strike destroys a building that U.S. Marines had identified as an insurgent stronghold during the Battle of Fallujah in November 2004.

made up of U.S., British, and Australian experts, began to inspect hundreds of sites. Although before the war the CIA had reported that Iraq might have stockpiles of nuclear, biological, and chemical weapons, the inspectors did not find any useable weapons.

On September 30, 2004, the Iraq Survey Group released its final report. It said that Iraq had not produced weapons of mass destruction since 1991, and possessed no WMD when it was invaded in March 2003. However, the ISG report said that Saddam had tried to preserve the knowledge and equipment needed to make the banned weapons, so that he could restart the programs once U.N. economic sanctions were lifted.

A second justification for the war—the link with terrorism—also proved to be weak. After the war investigators confirmed that there had never been a direct relationship between Iraq and al-Qaeda. The *9/11 Commission Report*, released in July 2004, declared that Iraq had nothing to do with the September 11 attack. After the Iraq War ended, however, terrorists flocked to Iraq to join the insurgency, and al-Qaeda used anger among Muslims at the U.S. invasion to recruit new members. As a

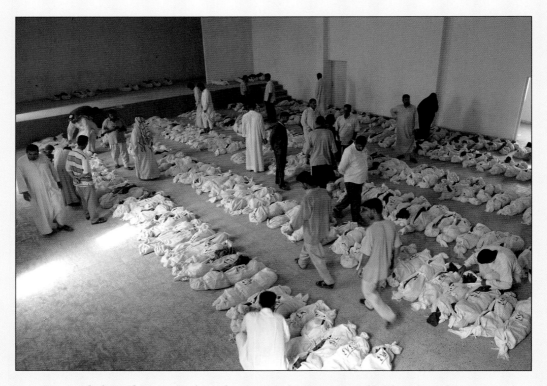

Iraqis search for relatives or friends among the remains of bodies found in a mass grave in Iraq during 2004.

result, many experts concluded that the occupation in Iraq actually increased the threat of global terrorism.

Although Bush and other U.S. leaders had been wrong about the threat that Iraq posed, they were tragically correct when they said that Saddam Hussein had cruelly mistreated the Iraqi people. After the war hundreds of mass graves were found, containing the bodies of more than 300,000 people murdered by the regime. Most were believed to be Shiites, Kurds, or opponents of the Baath Party.

Saddam Hussein managed to elude American troops for several months, but he was finally found on December 13, 2003, hiding in a tiny tunnel on a farm in Adwar, a town about 10 miles (16 km) from his hometown of Tikrit. A court called the Iraqi Special War Crimes Tribunal was formed during 2004 to hold trials for the dictator and other leading figures from his regime. In October 2005, Saddam and seven associates faced trial for crimes against humanity. After a yearlong trial, Saddam was found guilty and sentenced to death. On December 30, 2006, the former dictator of Iraq was hanged.

Fighting the Insurgency

American troops suffered thousands of casualties trying to bring order to Iraq. Bush administration officials hoped that turning the government over to Iraqis would end the violence. In January 2005, Iraqis voted for a transitional national assembly. In December of that year, following the adoption of a constitution, Iraqis went to the polls and voted for a permanent government.

Unfortunately, hopes that the elections would bring peace were soon dashed, and the violence in Iraq escalated during 2005. That spring, insurgents gained control over the city of Tal Afar, and in September 2005 a force of American and Iraqi soldiers mounted an offensive to take back the city. At Tal Afar, the U.S. military implemented a new strategy called "clear, hold, build." American soldiers would clear all the insurgents out of part of the city, establish outposts that would enable that area to be protected, and would then rebuild the infrastructure in that area. Once those

A U.S. Army Airborne sergeant breaches a courtyard door while searching for insurgents in Tal Afar.

things were complete, that part of the city could be turned over to Iraqi police forces and the U.S. military would move to another area and repeat the process.

During the fall of 2005, Abu Musab al-Zarqawi declared "all-out war" on Shiites in Iraq. He sent suicide bombers throughout Iraq to attack American soldiers and areas with large concentrations of Shiite militias. Sectarian violence increased after a bomb was detonated at the al-Askari Mosque in Samarra, one of the holiest Shiite shrines in Iraq, in February 2006.

With the fall of Fallujah to coalition forces in late 2004, Ramadi became the center of the insurgency in Iraq. In April of 2006, insurgent forces led by Zarqawi captured several important government buildings and attacked U.S. military bases and outposts. The U.S. military soon launched a campaign against the insurgents, although it tried to avoid the use of airstrikes and artillery bombardments that might result in civilian casualties. This required U.S. soldiers to patrol the streets, where they were often attacked by snipers or small groups of insurgents. The second battle of Ramadi lasted through the end of the year, and many experts

Two American soldiers lay down covering fire as their teammate launches a grenade (seen traveling through the air) at insurgents in Ramadi.

The decision by Sunni tribal leaders in Anbar province to work with the Iraqi government and U.S. military to oppose insurgents in the region enabled the military to clear and hold the region.

believed that Iraq was on the verge of a full-blown civil war.

There were positive signs, however. Zarqawi was killed in the summer of 2006, weakening the group's influence. More importantly, in August of 2006, Sunni tribal leaders in the western province of Anbar decided to stop fighting American forces. In return for monthly cash payments, the Iraqi Sunnis joined American soldiers in fighting back against the insurgents, particularly al-Qaeda in Iraq. This development, called the Anbar Awakening or the Sunni Awakening, gradually spread to other parts of Iraq.

The Surge Strategy Succeeds

In January 2007, the Bush administration announced a troop *surge*—an increase in American soldiers in Iraq, in order to stabilize the country. Over the next six months an additional 40,000 U.S. troops were sent to key areas such as Baghdad and the Anbar province in order to ensure that the "clear, hold, and build" strategy could be carried out. By September 2007, there were 170,000 American soldiers in Iraq.

Along with the surge in troops, there was also a change in U.S. tactics. The American soldiers would not be focused on traditional combat operations against insurgents. Instead, their goal would be what is known as counterinsurgency. The U.S. would sup-

General David Petraeus helped to develop counterinsurgency tactics that proved effective in Iraq when coupled with the troop surge.

port Iraq's military and police forces, but they would also provide jobs, facilitate reconstruction, and strive to reduce civilian casualties in order to maintain peace.

The combination of the Sunni Awakening and the changes in American strategy contributed to decreased levels of violence in Iraq, and hope that the conflict was finally near an end. Still, the prospects for a peaceful and stable Iraq hinged on political compromises among the country's Sunni, Shiite, and Kurdish groups.

By late 2008 the government of Prime Minister Nouri al-Maliki was confident enough in the progress toward stability to begin negotiating a security agreement with the United States by which all American troops would leave Iraq by the end of 2011. In early 2009 the newly elected U.S. president, Barack Obama, announced his intention to withdraw most American military forces from Iraq by August 2010, with all forces to be removed by 2011 in compliance with the Iraqi government's wishes. In December 2011 the last U.S. troops left the country and the war was declared over.

Conflict Continues in Iraq

Although the insurgency seemed to be under control by 2011, it would flare up again once American soldiers were withdrawn from Iraq. In part, the renewal of conflict in Iraq was spurred by uprisings in other Arab countries that began in late 2010 and early 2011. The anti-government protests, which became known as the Arab Spring, were aimed at improving the political circumstances and living conditions of the Arab people. In Tunisia and Egypt, protesters succeeded in overthrowing the governments. In Syria, which borders Iraq, protesters used marches, hunger strikes, rioting, vandalism, and guerrilla attacks in an attempt to overthrow the repressive government of President Bashar al-Assad. The uprising in Syria began in 2011, and soon turned into a full-scale civil war, with government forces attacking various Syrian armed factions and bombing cities.

In Iraq, Arab Spring protests began during early 2012, as Sunni Muslims boycotted the Shiite-dominated government, claiming that it was trying to minimize Sunnis. In addition, both Iraqi Sunnis and Shiites were galvanized by the Syrian civil war, and many militants from both sects crossed the border to fight in Syria.

During 2014 Sunni insurgents seized control of a large area of Iraqi territory, capturing major cities like Tikrit, Fallujah, and Mosul. The insurgents declared themselves to be part of a group called the Islamic State of Iraq and the Levant (ISIL), which declared itself to be a caliphate, or Islamic theocracy ruling over this territory.

As reports of ISIL atrocities committed against Christians, Kurds, and Shiite Muslims in Iraq and Syria were reported, the United States and other countries agreed to intervene with military force. Airstrikes were launched against ISIL positions, although the U.S. and other countries decided not to send in soldiers to wage ground combat. However, by the summer of 2015 American leaders were reconsidering the use of ground forces after ISIL routed the Iraqi Army and captured the important city of Ramadi. The future of Iraq remains uncertain, but it is clear that the United States will remain engaged in this region for many years to come.

 ## TEXT-DEPENDENT QUESTIONS

1. What Shiite cleric was the leader of the Mahdi Army?
2. What was the name of the transitional government set up by the United States after the fall of Saddam Hussein?
3. What were the conclusions of the Iraq Survey Group's final report, released in 2004?

 ## RESEARCH PROJECT

The organization ISIL has declared that it is forming a new caliphate—a theocracy in which all people must obey Islamic laws. Using the internet or your school library, find out more about ISIL. What are this organization's goals and objectives? What tactics has it used to accomplish these goals? Write a report and share it with your class.

Chronology

1979   Saddam Hussein becomes president of Iraq.

1980   Iraq invades Iran in September.

1987   Saddam Hussein begins attacking Iraqi Kurds; hundreds of thousands are killed or left homeless.

1988   A cease-fire ends the Iran-Iraq War; Iraq asks OPEC to increase its production quota.

1990   Tensions between Iraq and Kuwait rise, leading to Iraq's invasion on August 2. The United Nations condemns the attack. On November 29, the U.N. Security Council passes Resolution 678, which threatens military action if Iraq does not withdraw from Kuwait by January 15.

1991   The Gulf War begins on January 17 with a bombing campaign. After six weeks, a ground campaign begins. The Iraqi army is routed in 100 hours, and a cease-fire is declared. Saddam agrees to comply with U.N. resolutions requiring him to disarm. The coalition establishes a no-fly zone over northern Iraq to protect the Kurds from Saddam's forces.

1992   A second no-fly zone is established over the southern part of Iraq, to protect Shiites.

1995   An Iraqi defector tells UNSCOM inspectors about Saddam's secret biological weapons program. The program is destroyed.

1997   Iraq refuses to allow UNSCOM to inspect Saddam's palaces. Scott Ritter, an American member of UNSCOM, is accused of being a spy and is expelled from Iraq.

1998   The crisis over inspections culminates in Operation Desert Fox, a four-day bombing campaign.

2001   George W. Bush is inaugurated as president of the United States. On September 11, terrorists attack the World Trade

Center and Pentagon. In response, the U.S. launches its "war on terrorism" and attacks Afghanistan.

2002 The Bush Doctrine declares that the United States will use preemptive war when necessary to protect its interests. U.S. leaders urge the United Nations to force Iraq to comply with U.N. resolutions, and Bush administration officials begin planning for war. In November, the U.N. Security Council passes Resolution 1441, which offers Iraq a "final opportunity" to disarm. Saddam agrees to allow inspections to resume.

2003 Despite pressure from the United Nations, the United States, Britain, and their allies launch a war against Iraq on March 20. On April 9, Saddam and his government are forced to leave Baghdad as U.S. troops occupy the city. In December, Saddam is found hiding on a small farm and is captured.

2004 On June 28, the coalition hands over power to an interim Iraqi government. U.S. and British forces remain in the country, fighting a growing insurgency. On September 30, the Iraq Survey Group reports that Saddam did not possess weapons of mass destruction at the time Iraq was invaded.

2005 In January, Iraqis go to the polls to elect a new government. U.S. troops remain in Iraq, battling a violent insurgency.

2006 In February an important Shiite shrine, the Golden Mosque of Samarra, is bombed, igniting a wave of sectarian killings. In November Saddam Hussein is found guilty of crimes against humanity; he is executed in December.

2007 President Bush announces an American troop surge. The Sunni Awakening, which began in Anbar province, begins to spread. Violence in Iraq begins to subside.

2008 In November the Iraqi parliament approves an agreement by which American troops are to leave Iraq by the end of 2011.

2009 In June, U.S. troops begin to withdraw from Iraqi cities and villages.

2010   In January, Ali Hassan al-Majid, a key figure in Saddam Hussein's government who was nicknamed "Chemical Ali" for his use of chemical weapons against Iraq's Kurdish population during the 1980s, is executed. In August, the last U.S. combat brigade leaves Iraq.

2011   In December, the United States withdraws the last of its troops from Iraq.

2012   Terrorist attacks targeting Shia Muslims spark fears of a new sectarian conflict. Nearly 200 people are killed in January, more than 160 in June, 113 in a single day in July, more than 70 people in August, about 62 in attacks nationwide in September, and at least 35 before and during the Shia mourning month of Muharram in November. Thousands of Syrians flee to neighboring countries, including Iraq, to escape the civil war in that country.

2013   The insurgency in Iraq intensifies, and by June experts agree that the situation has become a civil war. The United Nations estimates that 7,157 civilians were killed during 2013, a significant increase over the 2012 figure of 3,238.

2014   In June, the Islamic State of Iraq and the Levant (ISIL) seizes Mosul and other key towns. Kurdish forces assist the Iraqi military in repelling attacks, with assistance from Iran and the United States.

2015   In January, terrorist bombings in Baghdad and Kirkuk, carried out by ISIL guerrillas, kill dozens of people. A U.S.-led military coalition continues to launch airstrikes against the Islamic State of Iraq and the Levant in support of Iraqi and Kurdish efforts to recapture Mosul. In May the city of Ramadi is captured by ISIL forces.

Chapter Notes

p. 11:   "graveyard" Saddam Hussein, quoted in Simon Tisdall and David Hirst, "Superpowers unite on Iraq," *The Guardian* (August 3, 1990). http://www.theguardian.com/century/1990-1999/Story/0,,112384,00.html?redirection=century

p. 25:   "no legal validity, ..." U.N. Security Council Resolution 662, August 9, 1990. http://www.un.org/en/ga/search/view_doc.asp?symbol=S/RES/662(1990)

p. 26:   "We call for the immediate ..." George H.W. Bush, "Remarks and an Exchange With Reporters on the Iraqi Invasion of Kuwait," August 2, 1990. http://www.presidency.ucsb.edu/ws/index.php?pid=18726&st=naked+aggression&st1=

p. 32   "It is obvious ..." William J. Clinton, "Remarks at the Pentagon in Arlington, Virginia." February 17, 1998. http://www.presidency.ucsb.edu/ws/index.php?pid=55483&st=Iraq&st1=inspectors

p. 33:   "designed to degrade ..." William J. Clinton, "Address to the Nation Announcing Military Strikes on Iraq," December 16, 1998. http://www.presidency.ucsb.edu/ws/index.php?pid=55414&st=Iraq&st1=inspectors

p. 39:   "We don't want the smoking gun ..." Condoleeza Rice, quoted in "Top Bush officials push case against Saddam," CNN.com, September 8, 2002. http://www.cnn.com/2002/ALLPOLITICS/09/08/iraq.debate

p. 39   "defend the national security ..." U.S. Congress Public Law 107-243, "Authorization for Use of Military Force Against Iraq Resolution of 2002," October 16, 2002. http://www.gpo.gov/fdsys/pkg/PLAW-107publ243/html/PLAW-107publ243.htm

p. 39   "Iraq continues to shelter ..." George W. Bush, "Address to the United Nations General Assembly in New York City," September 12, 2002. http://www.presidency.ucsb.edu/ws/index.php?pid=64069&st=Iraq&st1=terrorists

p. 40   "a final opportunity to comply ..." U.N. Security Council Resolution 1441, November 8, 2002. http://www.un.org/depts/unmovic/documents/1441.pdf

p. 40   "did not provide any new information ..." Mohamed ElBaradei, "The Status of Nuclear Inspections in Iraq," Statement to the United Nations Security Council, January 27, 2003. http://www.un.org/News/dh/iraq/elbaradei27jan03.htm

p. 41   ""Iraq appears not to have come ..." Hans Blix, "An Update on Inspection," Statement to the United Nations Security Council, January 27, 2003. http://www.un.org/Depts/unmovic/Bx27.htm

p. 41   "The issue before us ..." Colin Powell, "U.S. Secretary of State Colin Powell Addresses the U.N. Security Council," White House Press Office, February 5, 2003. http://georgewbush-whitehouse.archives.gov/news/releases/2003/02/20030205-1.html

p. 42   "At this hour, ..." George W. Bush, "President Bush Addresses the Nation," White House Press Office, March 19, 2003. http://georgewbush-whitehouse.archives.gov/news/releases/2003/03/20030319-17.html

p. 45:   "major combat operations." George W. Bush, "President Bush Announces Major Combat Operations in Iraq Have Ended" Remarks by the President from the USS Abraham Lincoln, White House Press Office, May 1, 2003. http://georgewbush-whitehouse.archives.gov/news/releas-es/2003/05/20030501-15.html

Further Reading

Arnold, James R. *Saddam Hussein's Iraq*. Brookfield, Conn.: Twenty-First Century Books, 2008.

Gallagher, Jim. *Causes of the Iraq War*. Stocktonm NJ: OTTN Publishing, 2007.

Haass, Richard N. *War of Necessity: A Memoir of Two Iraq Wars*. New York: Simon and Schuster, 2009.

Mansfield, Peter. *A History of the Middle East*. 4th ed. revised and updated by Nicholas Pelham. New York: Penguin Books, 2013.

Ricks, Thomas E. *The Gamble: General David Petraeus and the American Military Adventure in Iraq, 2006-2008*. New York: Penguin Press, 2009.

Stern, Jessica, and J.M. Berger. *ISIS: The State of Terror*. New York: Ecco, 2015.

Internet Resources

www.pbs.org/wgbh/pages/frontline/gulf

This site is a companion to the Frontline program "The Gulf War," with links to oral accounts from both decision-makers and ordinary soldiers, information about the 1990–91 Gulf crisis, and a detailed chronology.

www.foreignaffairs.com/articles/iraq/2007-01-01/united-states-iraq-and-war-terror

Links to an article in the journal Foreign Affairs titled "The United States, Iraq, and the War on Terror."

http://www.cnn.com/SPECIALS/2003/iraq

This collection of CNN reports and information about the 2003 Iraq War was archived when the president declared an end to major combat operations.

https://www.cia.gov/library/reports/general-reports-1/iraq_wmd_2004

The text of a 2004 CIA report, which found that Iraq did not possess weapons of mass destruction at the time the United States invaded in 2003.

http://www.un.org/News/

This website of the United Nations includes links to articles about current U.N. programs in Iraq.

Publisher's Note: The websites listed on this page were active at the time of publication. The publisher is not responsible for websites that have changed their address or discontinued operation since the date of publication. The publisher reviews and updates the websites each time the book is reprinted.

Index

Numbers in **bold italics** refer to captions.

SERIES GLOSSARY

blockade—an effort to cut off supplies, war material, or communications by a particular area, by force or the threat of force.

guerrilla warfare—a type of warfare in which a small group of combatants, such as armed civilians, use hit-and-run tactics to fight a larger and less mobile traditional army. The purpose is to weaken an enemy's strength through small skirmishes, rather than fighting pitched battles where the guerrillas would be at a disadvantage.

intelligence—the analysis of information collected from various sources in order to provide guidance and direction to military commanders.

logistics—the planning and execution of movements by military forces, and the supply of those forces.

salient—a pocket or bulge in a fortified line or battle line that projects into enemy territory.

siege—a military blockade of a city or fortress, with the intent of conquering it at a later stage.

tactics—the science and art of organizing a military force, and the techniques for using military units and their weapons to defeat an enemy in battle.